Tonka
PHONICS READING PROGRAM

W9-BUK-277

Book 2 - short e

Get Set to Wreck!

Written by Sonia Sander
& Illustrated by Rick Courtney

SCHOLASTIC INC.

New York   Toronto   London   Auckland   Sydney
Mexico City   New Delhi   Hong Kong   Buenos Aires

I am a crane.
I have a **wrecking** ball.
I do my **best** to make
a **mess**!

Let's get set to wreck!

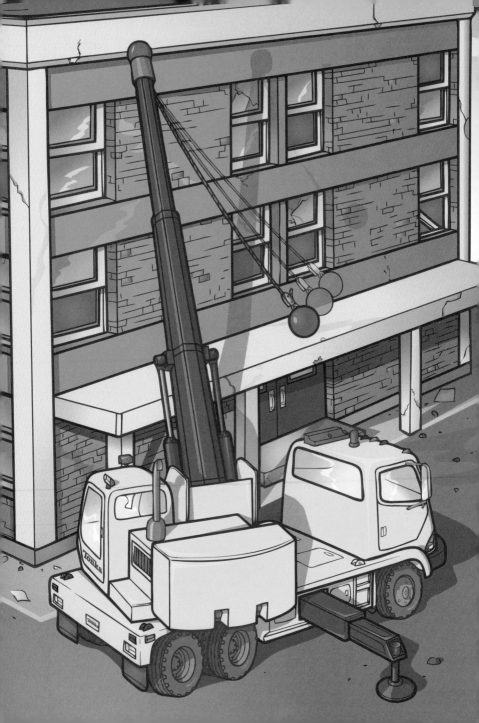

Let's send the metal ball flying.

Let's wreck the windows.

Then let's send the bricks into the air.

Next let's flatten
all the steps.

Let's get rid of the **rest.**

What can we **wreck next**?